THOMAS & FRIENDS™

The **Runaway Kite**

It was a **windy** day
on the Island of Sodor, perfect
weather for the Kite Festival!

The engines were excited.
And Thomas was the most
excited of all!

He **whooshed** along the track
with a huge smile on his face.

At the Docks, workmen carefully packed a trophy into a crate.

Cranky then loaded it into Thomas' carriage.

"Lady Hatt will present the trophy to the Kite Festival winner at tea time," The Fat Controller told Thomas.

Thomas saw a kite flying in the distance.

"Fizzling fireboxes! What a beautiful kite!" he said. "I hope I see it again."

When Thomas reached the top of Gordon's Hill, he saw that the kite was being flown by The Fat Controller's grandchildren, Stephen and Bridget.

Suddenly, a gust of wind blew the kite out of their hands. The children **gasped** as the kite flew away.

"Don't be sad!" said Thomas. "I'll get it back for you," he promised.

He forgot that he should be delivering the trophy to Knapford Station.

"I can help you follow the kite," Charlie told Thomas.

But Thomas thought he could do it by himself.

"No, thank you," he said. "I'm faster than you, so I'll chase it on my own."

Thomas *wheeshed* and *whooshed* as he chased the kite.

"I must keep up," he said, and he **chuffed** and **puffed** with all his might!

But then the kite flew around a corner and out of sight.

Emily, Percy and Edward
saw Thomas rushing after the kite.

They offered to help, but again
Thomas said no.

"I'm the fastest engine. I can
chase it by myself!"
he told them.

But when Thomas carried on, he **shuddered** and **juddered**, and then his boiler went out!

"Oh no!" he cried. "I'm **not** the fastest engine. I broke my promise to the children **and** I forgot to deliver the trophy!"

Thomas realised he needed some help after all.

Emily, Percy, Edward and Charlie agreed to help Thomas.

Charlie's Fireman loaded coal into Thomas' firebox so he could deliver the trophy to Knapford.

And Emily and the other engines **chased** after the kite.

Thomas met Stephen and Bridget
at Knapford Station.

"My friends are looking for your kite.
Why don't you come too?" he said.

Just as they met up with the engines, the kite
swooped down and caught on a signal!

"We've got it!"
smiled Thomas,
and the engines
tooted hooray!

Later that day, the sky was full of kites. And flying highest of all was Stephen and Bridget's kite.

The engines watched happily. The children's kite looked so beautiful that Thomas was sure it was going to win the trophy!

Can you see the children's kite?

PEEP! PEEP!

The End